THE GOBBLER CALLED

By the same author

THE TIME OF THE WOLVES

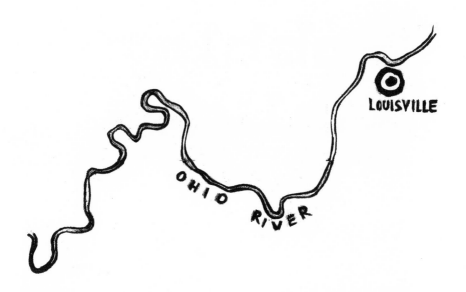

OHIO RIVER

LOUISVILLE

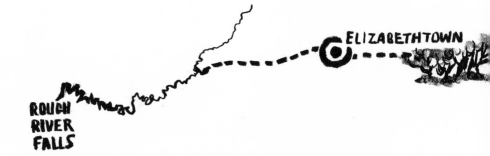

ELIZABETHTOWN

ROUGH
RIVER
FALLS

The Gobbler Called

HARRODSBURG

BOONESBORO

VERNE T. DAVIS

ILLUSTRATED BY EZRA JACK KEATS

WILLIAM MORROW & CO. • NEW YORK • 1963

CONTENTS

THE GOBBLER CALLED

1.
News from the West

Jan quickly closed the door of the little general store, and stood shaking the snow off his coonskin cap as he looked around. The men of the settlement, a small one called Boonsboro, were sitting on the counters, kegs, boxes, and the two chairs the store afforded.

"What brings you out, Jan?" his father, Tom Harris, inquired from his perch on the dry-goods counter.

Jan's father was sitting next to Tip Logan, with whom he had campaigned under Washington three years before when Cornwallis surrendered at Yorktown. Jan noted that the scout Trent Haskell, who had served under Washing-

11

ton too, was also present. He had often listened
to his father and his two friends talk over their
war experiences and Indian fighting since the
war. Jan said, "Mom wants you to bring home a
sack of flour." He handed a small bucket to
George Ball, the storekeeper. "She wants a
gallon of molasses too."

Mr. Ball opened the tap of the molasses barrel
and impatiently watched the thick, amber
stream slowly fill the bucket. Then he hastened
back to join in the always interesting discussion
of moving farther west. Making sales was of
secondary importance to conversation, so far as
Mr. Ball was concerned. His was probably the
most sloppily kept store between the Atlantic
coast and the Mississippi. The merchandise in
barrels, boxes, and on the few pine shelves pre-
sented a study in magnificent confusion.

Jan sat down to listen to Tip Logan, who
seemed to have the floor. "It's a wonderful
country," he was saying to the men. "Just ask
Trent here. He's been out that way. Plenty of
deer and elk feed in the timber and grassy bot-

toms. Some buffalo, too, though they're thicker farther west."

Jan noticed that Tip had a habit of looking down at his feet between bursts of speech, as though thinking over thoroughly what he would say next. Now he looked around at the faces of the dozen men who had established this settlement in what would later be called Kentucky. The store was a favorite loafing place on Saturday nights. The big box stove in the rear of the room, well stocked with walnut chunks, showed red hot as the heat waves overcame the cold outside.

"This place is getting too crowded for me," Tip continued. "If you people want to move a hundred miles or so west, me'n Trent will take you through. We can start in April. There won't be any big rivers to cross the way we'll take you. What do you say, Trent?"

"You've said it pretty well," Trent Haskell agreed. "I'll go." He shifted his six feet of hardened muscles on the empty keg, and tapped his pipe against the sandbox the stove was set in.

Trent wasted few words. His face, like Tip Logan's, was tanned and weather-beaten, and their years of rough experience made them look older than their age of forty-five.

Jan knew his father was interested in moving farther west, so he was surprised to hear him say, "That's getting pretty far into hostile territory." The Harrises had moved to Boonsboro as soon as the war had ended. Jan's father still limped as the result of a musket ball in his leg, received in a late skirmish of the war, but his itchy feet were always tempted by the lure of unsettled territory further on.

The gathering soon broke up, but Jan mulled the proposal over in his mind before going to sleep. The next morning, over a leisurely Sunday breakfast, Jan introduced the subject of moving on. With a diffident glance at his buxom, energetic mother, he said, "The first bunch to get there would have the pick of the land."

"There is plenty of unsettled land right around here," Molly Harris put in, at once on the defensive, before her husband had time to answer. "We've lived on the edge of civilization the whole sixteen years since Katie was born. You know Katie and Terry Seaton plan to marry as soon as she is seventeen, and that time isn't far away. We aren't going traipsing off and split up the family. And you, Jan, need another year of school, at the least."

"Russ Seaton is in favor of making the move, too," Mr. Harris said. "And if Russ and Cora go, Terry and Norie will go with them."

They dropped the subject as Katie came down the ladder from the room above. But Jan, when his plate was heaped high with sausage and hot cakes, brought it up again. "I'd like to shoot some elk and buffalo," he said. "They were mostly killed off or run out when we first came here."

"I like this place," Katie spoke up. "You do too, don't you, Mom? The more people come here to stay, the more work there will be for everyone."

"You're thinking about how much work Terry will have as a carpenter," Jan said. "That's all you two will ever care about. No imagination. I'll bet you'll be a nice old married couple five years after the wedding."

"That will be plenty, Jan," his mother cut in. "Too bad you don't take as much interest in work as you do in hunting. That seems to be all that interests you."

Jan's father spoke up in defense of him. "You

know, Molly, some have to be good with a rifle or there wouldn't be any settlers—just Indians. At thirteen, he can outshoot half the men in Boonsboro, and he's turned out to be a pretty good tracker, too."

"I know all that," Mrs. Harris admitted. She gave her husband an approving slap on the back on her way to the stove to pour another batch of batter on the griddle. "He's just like his father. He'd rather shoot his food than raise it."

2.

The
Departure

Like bees that swarm in the spring and go forth to establish a colony of their own, the settlers of early America seemed to be always moving westward. The contagion generated by Tip Logan spread to every cabin in the village. Two weeks after the session in Ball's store, a meeting was called for discussion. Nobody was quite sure who had called the meeting, but half the adults packed themselves into the largest of the two churches in town.

Tip stood behind a small table beside the pulpit to make his talk. "I guess you all are interested in making a move to the west," he began. "I've talked to about every man present

18

the past few days about the location I believe is perfect for a settlement. Now I'll answer any questions you have."

Heindrich Hoffer, towering six feet six, stood up. "I have a big family of eight kids, as you all know," he said. "But I am a good blacksmith. One good blacksmith is needed in any place."

"We need men with rifles, Mr. Hoffer," Tip told him.

"My son, John, is nineteen and Chris is seventeen," Mr. Hoffer said. "They are both good with rifles. Connie is not yet sixteen, but she shoots the shotgun well. I, too, use the shotgun. I am not good with guns, but I can make on my anvil fine hammers and triggers for broken guns, hinges for doors, and sharpen plowpoints."

"I could take my two horses," one man volunteered.

"We could use a few horses for plowing and snaking in logs for the blockhouse we'll have to build," Tip agreed.

Many matters were discussed. Either Tip Logan or Trent Haskell seemed qualified to furnish the answers. Jan noticed that his father's opinion was frequently asked too. The army experience of the three was respected. At the end of the discussion, Tip produced paper and ink. Those who had fully decided to join the venture signed with the quill pen. Many were still undecided. Jan's father, after a brief talk with his mother, refrained from signing. Jan was deeply disappointed. He knew his father had been using all his powers of persuasion to get his mother to decide favorably on the move, but evidently he had not succeeded. Jan resolved he would insist upon being heard on the matter when they reached home.

Tip issued a final warning. "Nobody should start on this trip if they have any doubts whatsoever. It will be rough. We'll be in danger from Indians every step of the way, and after we get settled, too. People with small children should think plenty about the hardship and danger. We'll be strictly on our own. Think it over."

Jan mulled everything over as the family walked home. As soon as they left their neighbors, he opened up his attack. "Dad," he said, "you didn't sign up tonight. Aren't we going?"

"Ask your mother, Jan," was his father's brief reply.

The uncompromising expression upon his mother's face did not encourage argument, but Jan decided this would be his last opportunity to change her mind. He hurried on. "All the best land close to town here has been bought up. We'll never get ahead here, but out where the party is heading the land is open for homesteading. Don't you think we should go, Mom, while we have a good, strong party to travel with?"

The set expression of disapproval on Mrs. Harris's face softened as she listened to her son's urgent plea. She replied gently, "I know, Jan, how you feel about this. Most men are the same —always ready to move on to some new land of promise. But women think more of the danger and hardship. We like to plant our feet on some spot that will continue to be home. Do you understand, Jan?"

Jan could muster no further words. He draped his arm around his mother's shoulders, and said, "I'll say no more about it, Mom."

"That goes for me, too, Molly," Tom Harris said. "We'll just forget about it."

But reinforcements came from the most unexpected quarter. Katie, who had taken no part in the conversation, spoke up with a troubled voice. "Mr. Seaton signed up to go. When I talked with Terry tonight, he said he would go with the family. Said he would come back to get me next year, but I don't know. Traveling alone through Indian country is too dangerous for two people like us. If I don't go with him now, we may never get together." She turned away to hide the tears trickling down her face.

Molly Harris broke a long silence. "Perhaps I'm selfish," she said. "After all, there seem to be three opinions against one. Sign up tomorrow, Tom. They'll be mighty pleased to have two more good rifles on the trail. But remember this —there will be no more moves for the Harris family."

A month later practically every inhabitant of the settlement turned out to see the start of the expedition. The spring day was bright and warm. Traditionally, most ventures of this kind took off in the spring, so that the adventurers had time to get well settled before winter.

The party was made up of nine complete families, plus Tip Logan, Trent Haskell, and Grandpa Clem, seventy, but still active. He wore no glasses and his greatest worry was whether he could carry enough chewing tobacco to last till he could raise a crop. Morris Albretch, a young man of twenty-four, completed the list.

At the last meeting of the pioneers, Trent Haskell had expressed his views concerning a leader. "Somebody has to head this bunch," he declared. "I nominate Tip. Anybody have a better idea?"

No one spoke. "In that case," Trent said, "I'll call myself chairman for a couple of minutes while we take a vote. Everyone answer when I call his name." He called the name of everyone old enough to carry a gun. There were no dissenting votes. "Tip is in command," he declared. "We may argue a little, but what he says goes."

Now Jan followed Tip Logan about as he went over the things the members of the party had brought to the meeting place on the main street of the town. He observed that Tip was ruthlessly weeding out everything he considered unnecessary, consulting with Trent Haskell and his father when he had any doubt about his judgment.

"These two flatirons, Mrs. Tyndal," he said to a young wife, carrying a six-months-old babe in her arms, "we can get along without. Probably weigh four pounds apiece. Eight pounds of powder would do us a heap more good." He sized up Terry Seaton's pack, consisting of his carpenter tools in a flat box on his back and a hundred feet of three-quarter-inch Manila rope looped around his shoulders. "Nothing wrong with your pack, Terry, if you can carry it a hundred miles," he approved.

Tip finally stepped up onto the big log that had been hollowed out for a horse trough. "Listen to me," he yelled. "We may as well get something straight right now. What you carry isn't just your private business. Everything must be figured for the good of the whole party. We're starting with four horses. These horses will pack our food and cooking utensils. This plow that Dick Burdick wants to take along will be used for the good of all of us. We'll pack it on one of the horses along with this forty pounds of lead for molding bullets. Fill your powder horns to the limit. Now we've fooled around here so long trying to get things straightened out for a start that it's nearly noon. Go back and throw away anything you can't carry on your backs, and be ready tomorrow morning to start without any more fuss."

Jan heard Pete Simpson, the shoemaker, chuckle as the gathering broke up. "Old Tip will tell 'em off and make 'em like it. Bet they'll be rid of all those things when they show up in the morning."

This proved to be the case. Nevertheless, Heindrich Hoffer showed up with his anvil in a kind of leather sling strapped to his back. "This we must have," he declared. Apparently an existence without an anvil, even though it weighed more than a hundred pounds, was unthinkable. Three of his children carried small bundles of strap iron along with a rolled-up blanket.

Everyone carried a pack of his most necessary possessions and supplies. Mrs. Harris carried, along with other things, one of the small kegs of powder being taken along. She looked over the pack Jan carried in addition to the small bore rifle that seemed a part of him. "Lucky you're big for your age, Jan," she observed with a smile.

As the time for departure neared, Tip Logan and Jan's father checked the hitches on the pack horses. Trent checked the firearms. "Fifteen rifles, three shotguns, and three pistols," he reported to Tip. "Not bad for forty-two people."

"I can't think of anything more to see to," Tip decided. "Let's line up and get going." Once more he mounted the horse trough. Everyone became quiet, realizing they were about to take the first step on their journey.

"Now listen to this," Tip said. "This will be a dangerous trip into Indian territory. If anyone here wants to pull out now, I won't blame them, but once on the way there will be no turning back." He paused a moment while he looked over the upturned faces. No one answered.

"All right then," he continued. "Those leading the cattle and horses keep to the middle of the column. Trent Haskell and Tom Harris will stay to the rear, and I'll be up in front. Better stay up there with me, Jan."

Jan flushed with satisfaction as he ranged himself alongside of Tip. This was a distinction he hadn't expected.

The townspeople who had come out to see them off let out a resounding yell as the little cavalcade moved away up the street, waving at friends and, in some cases, relatives they were leaving behind. Many of the well-wishers who lined the unpaved street had brought their rifles, and now they fired a farewell salute. Young

Howard Tyndal pointed his rifle toward the sky and fired an answer.

Tip held up his hand to halt the column. He walked back to Howard, and said pointedly, "Save your powder for the Indians. You'll probably need it." He regained his place at the head of the line, and the small party filed quietly up the street and out of town.

3.
Attack by the River

Their third night out was spent in Harrodsburg. The settlement was thirty miles west of Boonsboro and had been settled a year earlier. Its substantial blockhouse had withstood several Indian assaults. The people of the settlement made a gala occasion of the one night the party stopped inside their stockade. A party of this size had never passed through before.

The first night out from Harrodsburg, Tip called a halt beside a small creek when the sun was still high above the treetops. "From here on," he told his charges, "we'll be traveling through hostile territory. We'll start early and stop early in order to scout the territory where we camp. You may as well learn to keep quiet as we move. Tone the children down, and don't do any shouting. Now take off your packs and rest. We'll eat before dark, and sentinels will be posted through the entire night."

He turned to Trent. "Better do a little scouting a mile or two ahead, and you, Morris," to the blond young man, "do the same to the north. You bachelors haven't any family work to take care of. I'll take a run to the south. Tom, you and Jan stand guard here at camp. Someone else can do your work. This will be the procedure every day when we camp."

Later that evening, around the campfire, Trent told the party about the route they were taking. "I was through this territory two years ago," he said. "Mostly the Shawnees live to the north. But you may as well make up your mind to this: any redskin you see out this way is a bitter enemy of the likes of us. And we're bound to run into some before we finish the trip. Anyone on sentry duty had better take his job seriously. Don't move around, and keep a close watch for any movement. Early dawn is their favorite time for attack—when there is just enough light so they can see. Mostly, travelers like us are still in their blankets.''

The party could not cover many miles a day. Smaller children had to be carried part of the time, but five-year-olds and older children walked the entire distance. The Tyndals took turns carrying their baby. They didn't consider it strange that they should start so hazardous a journey with a babe of six months.

Two cows and a yearling bull had been brought along. The cows were fresh and would give milk for many months. Like the horses, they snatched at the greenery as they traveled, and grazed where camp was made on the new growth carpeting the forest floor and the grass that had sprung up in open spots. Feed would become more abundant as the season advanced. The herd of seven animals would be a hindrance if the party suffered a direct attack, but the risk was worth it.

Forty-two people required much food. Tip

sometimes took Ed Thomas with him as he ranged ahead of the party, or sent him with Jan's father or Trent Haskell when they made the evening scout. Ed had brought along a bow and a quiver full of arrows. Mr. Hoffer had made the steel heads in his blacksmith shop in Boonsboro. He pulled a strong bow and kept the party in meat. It wasn't safe now to use a gun for hunting. Jan resolved that he would acquire more skill with a bow. He had learned to use one in Boonsboro, but not well enough to hunt deer.

On the sixth day, a halt was made on the bank of a stream big enough to be called a river. "This, folks, is it for today," Tip announced. "We're about forty miles from the falls. That's the place we've been aiming for. Better take the north scout today, Tom," he directed. "Stay here and keep guard on the camp with Jan, Morris. I'll paddle a log across the stream and take a look up and down the river while Trent takes a look to the south on this side. Indians have a habit of following rivers."

In half an hour Trent came hurrying back.

He took a look around to make sure Morris and Jan were on guard. The party gathered around him. "What's the matter, Trent?" one of the women asked. They sensed that something was wrong.

"I cut the trail of a big band of Indians, maybe thirty," he told them. "There were no squaw moccasin tracks. They came from across the river and were traveling north. If they keep on in that direction, we're all right. If not, we're in for trouble. How long has Tip been gone?"

"Left right after you did," Jan told him.

"I wish he and Tom would get back," Trent said. Then, taking charge, he ordered, "All men with rifles scatter out a couple of hundred feet from camp and form a line around it. John and Chris," he said to the Hoffer boys, "stay here and keep an eye on the river. Warn Tip when he shows. You women gather some wood, but don't go beyond the men. Norie and Connie keep your shotguns in your hands and keep the small children together. Tie the horses and cattle to trees so they won't get in the way if trouble starts. If nothing happens in the next half-hour, we may figure they've passed on."

Everyone sprang to do Trent's bidding, and he went out among the men to make sure they were properly concealed. Jan was well hidden behind a big oak. Trent had scarcely finished his rounds, when a shot was heard a little way to the north. "Tom!" Trent exclaimed. "You men stay put," he ordered those nearest him. "Pass the word down the line, and keep quiet. Morris come with me."

Trent and Morris started swiftly away in the direction of the sound of the shot. Jan sprang forward. "Let me go too, Trent," he said. "Dad may be hurt. You might need more help."

"You can come a little way," Trent answered, without breaking his stride.

A moment later Jan saw his father. "Here comes Dad," he cried. "He's running as if he's hurt."

"Stop here, Jan, and get behind a tree," Trent ordered, but he and Morris continued on. Peeking from behind his tree, Jan saw his father stumble by Trent and Morris, who had also stepped behind trees. Then he saw a group of Indians pursuing him, seemingly intent upon taking him alive. Shots from the rifles ahead rang out, and the Indians ceased yelling and disappeared behind trees. They were still too far away for Jan to see what damage had been done. "Keep going, Dad," he said, as his father painfully made his way by him, an arrow in his back.

Now the rifles of Trent and Morris were empty, so they started retreating from tree to tree. The Shawnees were fast shortening the distance between them. Jan drew on one who was well in the lead, and the red man went down with the shot. Jan did not tarry. His shot had

slowed the Indians up enough to ease the pressure on Trent and Morris, and the three of them managed to retreat behind the line of the pioneers' rifles.

Now the Shawnees threw all caution aside. As far as they knew, three men with empty rifles were ahead of them. With wild yells they dashed in pursuit, and the guns of the riflemen began speaking. Four Indians, seeing the women and children bunched together, dashed right into camp. A blast from Norie's shotgun cut one down, and Connie accounted for another. Hoffer fired his shotgun and missed his man. He proved, indeed, that he was not good with guns. Dropping his gun, he picked up a six-foot pole that had been cut for hanging the kettle and brought it down with crushing force upon the head of an Indian, whose bow was full drawn with the arrow pointed at the big Dutchman. Without a pause, he swung it hard against the back of the last Indian, whose tomahawk was poised above the head of one of the women, as she was protecting two crying children with her skirts. As he fell with a broken back, Hoffer finished him with another blow on the head.

The firing ceased. Those attackers still alive darted away into the forest. Trent hurriedly made a check of the riflemen. He sent Cal Williams back to where the women and crying children were gathered. An arrow was stuck in Cal's shoulder. One other casualty was a bullet wound in the fleshy part of John Hoffer's leg. He had dashed from his place on the river back to camp when the shooting had started. He was sent in, also.

Tip appeared on the opposite bank of the river. Hearing the firing, he had hurried back. "Go cover him while he crosses," Trent ordered two of the men, "just in case some Indians are hanging around."

Jan now went in search of his father. He found his mother kneeling beside him, tucking a blanket under his head as he lay on his side gasping for breath. Jan knelt opposite her and ripped back the shirt to expose the wound from which the shaft of the arrow protruded. The head was buried deep in the corded muscles of his back, just under his shoulder.

Trent joined them and looked the injury over. "We'll have to get this out, Tom," he told him.

"Don't know as it matters much one way or another," Tom tiredly replied. "I'm bleeding inside. Bad place for an arrow. Better just leave it alone, it doesn't matter."

Mrs. Harris was struggling to hold her composure, but at her husband's words the tears started to flow. Her voice choked up as she tried to speak. Jan, his eyes burning in a dead white face, looked up at Trent and the men around them. "Is there some chance that Dad will live if the arrow is taken out?" he asked.

"The only chance," Trent answered.

Jan looked at his mother. Clearly she was in no condition to make such an important decision. He must shoulder the responsibility. "Take the arrow out," he told Trent and Tip, who had just come up. Then to Katie, who was kneeling beside her mother, "Take Mom away, Katie. Get those linen pads and bandages in the pack ready, and bring them and the turpentine to dress the wound when we call you."

Katie raised her mother to her feet and led her, sobbing, away.

Trent and Tip conferred quietly off to one side. Both had seen plenty of wounds and the crude surgery of the times as practiced in the army. Tip spoke to Jan. "Pulling this arrow back out would be sure death. The barbs would tear the flesh wide open. We'll cut the shaft off where it entered, and push it on through. It's almost through already." He knelt beside Jan, slid his hunting knife from its sheath, and cut a notch around the shaft, so he could snap it off.

Jan moved around to the opposite side. He patted his father's cheek, as he said, "I'm with you, Dad. It won't be but a moment." His lips moved in a little silent prayer.

"Help Trent hold him so he doesn't move," Tip told Heindrich Hoffer. "Now, Jan, when I push the arrow through, pull it on out."

Tip gave the shaft a quick shove. Jan seized the flint tip, protruding several inches beyond

Tom's chest, and gently drew it through. He was fighting with all his strength to keep control of himself.

As though from a long way off, he heard Trent's voice call, "Bring the bandages, Katie." His head cleared and he saw Tip looking at his father's face. "He's fainted," Tip said.

4.

By Land
or by
Water

Nightfall found all but the sentinels gathered around the central campfire, as usual. Tip had directed the women to prepare supper. "Work will settle you down," he told them, "and we'd better eat in peace while we can."

"There's just one thing I won't stand for," Cora Seaton said. "I won't use this pole for swinging the kettle. It's done its duty. Someone cut another."

Morris and Jan dragged the four dead Indians out of camp. "There are eight more out in the woods," Morris reported. "With the four shot before the ambush, they add up to sixteen."

"They're not likely to make a direct attack again," Tip said, "with half the band wiped out.

They'll gather reinforcements, no doubt, but it will take them a few days to do that. We can be sure, though, that we'll be watched."

All the bows and arrows found on the dead Indians were brought in. "Better bring in their moccasins, too," Trent suggested. "Some of the

least worn ones might come in handy before we
get around to making more footgear."

Later, when he looked over the collection of
moccasins, he said, "All Shawnees. Their women
make good moccasins. We had better burn all
those we don't want, and the bows and arrows,
too, so they won't pick them up after we're
gone."

"This strongest bow, I will keep," Heindrich
Hoffer said, picking up one from the heap. He
fitted an arrow to the string and sent it flying out

across the river. "I will practice much and learn to shoot straight. With this I shall shoot better than with the gun." He picked two quivers full of the best arrowheads.

Jan came from the shadows beyond the firelight, where he had been sitting with his mother and Katie. "Tip," he said, "Dad wants to talk to you and Trent." The two followed him back to the spot where Tom Harris lay on his blanket.

"Sorry I can't be up and taking part in your council," he said, when Tip and Trent had squatted in typical woodsman fashion beside him. "Jan just gave me an idea that is worth considering. This band of Shawnees will hang close to your line of travel from now on. They won't make an open attack, but they'll cause you a lot of trouble and slow you down. They may duck in and out and kill some of the party. The faster you travel, the less trouble you can expect to have."

He paused and rested a minute. His breathing was labored and painful. Gathering strength, he went on. "You might build two big rafts and float down the river. With so many men on the rafts, a close lookout could be maintained. You would move much faster and would get to the falls in a third the time. Go back and talk it over."

He rested again, then said tiredly, "Jan, bring me my rifle."

When Jan put it into his hands, he cradled it as one might a child. "There's no better rifle on the frontier than this, Jan," he said. "It's accurately sighted and has served me well. When I'm through with it, it will be yours, boy. You have keen sight and a steady nerve. A good rifle for a good marksman. Now go back and sit at the council fire."

The discussion about building rafts had begun when Jan took a seat in the circle around the fire. Tip seemed undecided as to the advisability of floating down an open river with no protection except their rifles. "I keep remembering the guns some of the Shawnees are carrying," he said. "And we'd be well in range of their arrows, where the brush is thick on the banks."

Trent was inclined to take a somewhat opposite view. "The same would hold true if we
were traveling on land," he said. "We're in for
trouble either way. How long will it take us to
build the rafts?"

Young Terry Seaton spoke up. "There are
plenty of trees right here, handy to the river," he
said. "Fastening them together won't be easy,
though. Maybe we can use some of the wild
grapevines. I have a two-inch auger in my toolbox. We can bore holes and fasten the logs together with dowels shaved round with a sharp
ax. There are fifty spikes in the toolbox, too. I
think it might be better to build three rafts and
string them together. We can build them a little
narrower than if we have only two, and they'll
take the curves in the river better."

The matter was thoroughly discussed, and the
decision was to build the rafts. "Cal and John
can stand guard, even if their wounds won't let
them work," Tip said. "So can Norie and Connie. I'd hate to have either one of them pointing
a charge of buckshot at me, if I were a red man.

That will leave eleven men to work, with some help from the women. Two days should see us ready to float."

Trent had something to say about organizing the work. "Eleven men will have eleven ideas about building a raft," he said. "One man should be in charge. I say Terry should have entire say about this building operation. He has never built a raft, but he has built other things, and his ideas are good."

All agreed that Terry should boss the raft building. Submitting themselves to the direction of a young man of nineteen seemed only sensible to the older men. The full potential must be squeezed from each individual to promote the welfare of the entire party.

"I'll do the best I can," Terry agreed modestly.

Katie, very proud of her future husband, came over and sat close to his side, with her hand on his shoulder.

Tall, orange-haired Mrs. MacGregor had something to say. "In Scotland we had the blessin' of peace, though the porridge was not always plentiful on the table. When I left with Colin there, we thought we were comin' to a land of plenty and a life of greater ease. But this is not the promised land to which we go. All is labor and killin'. The wilderness is full of savage red men, and we are but few. I say, let us forget the rafts. Let us turn back while there is still time. Soon we would be back in a land where one can walk about without the dread of feelin' an arrow in the back. I pray you, turn back when the daylight comes."

Surprised silence gripped the company as the Scotswoman finished her plea. Tip sat with lowered head. Then, speaking slowly and thoughtfully, he answered her. "It was well impressed upon everyone that there would be danger aplenty while making this journey, and more when we reached the place where we would settle. You should have listened to all the talk and warnings then, Mrs. MacGregor. We can't turn back, and no one here will be permitted to do so. You would be in the hands of the Shawnees before you were a mile upon your way. We'll all go on as planned."

Jan rose as his mother came into the circle. "Tom has quit breathing," she said. "He's dead."

5.

Building the Rafts

Daylight found all the adults up and attending to their duties. After a hurried breakfast, the men started cutting the trees Terry chose from those nearest the river. While a grave was dug, Mrs. Harris and Katie did their share of work with the other women, trying not to look at the blanket covering the still form. Pioneer women, conditioned by the perilous times, accepted tragedy when it came their way. Jan threw himself into the work to forget his grief and added responsibility as head of the family.

"The lead raft must be the best we can build," Terry explained. "It may bump into the bank on sharp curves and against trees or rocks in the river."

The main current of the river flowed against the opposite bank as it rounded the curve, so the water was shallower and not so swift at their side where they rolled the logs into the river. The men worked in water up to their waists, keeping the logs in place. Three strips were hewed out and laid flat across the top of the logs. Terry bored holes through the slabs and into the logs. Two men made round dowels to fit the two-inch auger holes. When they were driven through the slab and deep into the logs, the raft became quite rigid.

But Terry was not satisfied. "We can't go wrong by making it as strong as we possibly can," he declared. "Katie, you and Mrs. Mac-Gregor pull down some grapevines," he ordered. "Just the young and pliable ones. Take a hatchet along. We'll weave them over and under the logs and fasten them down, here and there, with a spike."

At noon they paused to lay Tom Harris in his wilderness grave. Mrs. Williams read from the little Bible she carried and offered a prayer. Her father had been a minister, and the few words she said were appropriate. Jan and Katie put their arms around their mother as sobs shook her frame.

"We'll take care of you, Mom," Jan told her.

No slab would mark Tom's forest grave. Trent and Morris tamped down the loose dirt and removed all traces that would indicate someone had been buried. Leaves that carpeted the floor of the surrounding woods were laid over the soil, and a small tree was cut down so the leafy top covered the spot.

"The less the Shawnees know about what has happened here, the better," Tip said.

Nothing was seen or heard of the enemy throughout the day. "You may be sure they know what's going on," Trent said, "even if they give no sign."

The end of the second day saw the finish of all the rafts. The lead raft was linked to the middle one with a length of the new Manila rope, leaving a three-foot space between to allow for flexibility of movement around the bends in the river.

"It hurts me to do this," Terry said, as he chopped off the fifteen-foot length from the coil. "We'll need this rope later on. I think we'd better use that chain we brought along for snaking in logs to fasten the middle and last raft together. We need the rest of the rope at the rear end of the rafts, so we can stop and tie up to a tree."

A sort of pen with walls two feet high was built around the edges of the middle raft. "All the women with children will ride this raft," Tip told them. "They can lie flat if we are attacked—and we will be."

The upstream raft was warped close to the bank. It would carry the stock. "I think," Tip said to Tyndal, who owned two of the horses, "we should get the stock used to the raft. We might lead them on and off a time or two."

The cattle made no trouble. There were enough men to push them on board, where they were tied to a rail that had been provided. One dappled gray of Tyndal's span reared and plunged, but was finally hazed aboard.

"Better do that all over again," Trent suggested. "We don't want any delay when we're ready to take off."

The entire company had put in two strenuous days, but they were optimistic about their safety on the river. They relaxed over the evening meal, though sentries were kept on guard.

When the camp was shrouded in darkness, Trent edged away from the fire. Two hours later he returned as silently as he had departed. The women and children were all asleep. He joined the men around the fire and told them what he had seen. "There's a Shawnee camp some distance from here with ten men. Probably they've sent a couple of braves off to get help, while the ten left will make us all the trouble they can when we start to move."

"Now listen carefully, you men," Tip said in a low tone, so the sleepers would not be disturbed. "A full moon will be up about midnight. We won't wait for morning to start down the river, but will load the stock and cast off then. We'll be taking a chance of bumping into something, perhaps, but it will be worth the gamble. If nothing delays us, we'll be so far ahead of the Shawnees when they discover we're gone that they'll never catch up till we've reached the falls. There we'll be better situated to defend ourselves."

When the moon rose above the treetops, the camp was flooded with sufficient light to make the operation of loading the rafts easy. The women were quietly awakened. "Keep the little ones asleep in their blankets," Jan whispered to each one. He had been given the office of arousing them and explaining what was about to take place.

The women and children filed aboard the rear raft and crossed the gap to the middle one. The stock, as anticipated, gave little trouble, except for the dappled gray that had acted up in the evening. Tyndal kept a close grip on the bridle. When it started to give a startled snort, his ready

fingers clamped down on its nostrils. Tyndal
knew his horses.

In thirty minutes everything was on the rafts.
The precious kegs of powder were lashed to the
posts of the protecting walls around the women's
raft, well above water. Tip took a last look
around. "I'll bring in the sentries," Trent said.

Terry untied the rope that was fastened to the last raft in the string, leaving several turns around the tree. After Trent had stepped on board, he let the rope go and followed him. The tug of the current slipped the rope from the tree, and they were free and afloat—for better or for worse.

Terry gathered in the trailing rope, hand over hand, and left it in a neat coil, ready for use when it should be needed again.

6.

Afloat on the River

As the string of rafts swung out to the middle of the stream, they gained momentum. Four men stood at the front end of the lead raft with poles, ready to fend it away from the bank or any obstruction in the water.

"I threw some chips into the water yesterday," Trent said, "and timed them. I figure the water is moving about as fast as a man can walk—four miles per hour. If we keep going, we should be fifteen miles from here by daylight."

But they were not to be so fortunate. An hour before daylight, the lead raft hung up in a brushy jam caused by driftwood that had gathered around a boulder jutting out of the water. The

rear end swung over against the bank. Terry
sprang ashore and wrapped the tail rope around
a tree near the edge of the river, so the raft would
be under control, and the current couldn't catch
it broadside.

Tip sized the situation up quickly. "The front
end of the logs have slid up onto this rock a
couple of feet. We'll have to back them up or
shove them off sideways. We'll have to cut all the
brush and driftwood loose and try to pry the raft
off into the water."

Two hours later the jam had been cleared
away. Young Chris Hoffer and Jan had re-
peatedly dived under the end of the raft to loosen
chunks and brush that pressed against the bottom. The men tried to pry the raft off with short
poles against the rock, but there was little space
where they could set the poles against its surface.

Trent had taken up his rifle and retired to the
bank. Time was running out on them. "If we
don't get this loose soon," Tip said, "we're going
to have that mess of Shawnees on our hands."

The men worked feverishly, but in another

half hour they had moved the raft only a few inches to one side.

"Morris," Trent called, "better come with me a little way up the river, so we can give some warning if the Indians overtake us. They could get here most any time. Indians are good runners."

"If we are overtaken," Tip said, "we'll have to back into the woods. Sitting out here in the open, we'd be whittled down, one at a time."

Chris, still working in the water, had a suggestion. "This water comes only to my armpits when I stand on the bottom. If some of you men would drop in here and lift, while others pried against the rock, we might do some good."

His father, with his great strength, was the first in the water. The raft moved with their exertions, but not enough.

Jan ran to the rear. "Let's try this, Tip," he said. "All you women come over to stand on this raft," he told them. "Hurry! You can jump the three feet between the rafts."

The weight of the women had the effect Jan

had hoped for. The front end rose slightly as the rear end settled down. The men at the front heaved with all their strength, and the raft slid slowly off the boulder, floating free.

As soon as it was clear, it started downstream and took up the slack in the rope. All the men in the water hooked their elbows over the logs and were helped up by those above—all but Heindrich Hoffer. The raft slid over him as it drifted. "I'm caught," he cried, just before his head disappeared.

Chris dived in and swam under the raft. His father was caught by a branch of a small tree and was fighting frantically to disentangle himself. Chris caught the branch with both hands, and bracing his feet against the logs, straightened out with all his strength. The branch cracked, and Heindrich was free. Seizing his father, Chris kicked out from under the logs. As the men hauled them aboard, with Heindrich gasping for breath, a shot was heard up the river. Then two more shots came, spaced half a minute apart.

Tip herded the women back onto the center

raft. "Lie down with the children," he ordered. The men snatched up their rifles. Norie and Connie sprang for their guns, also.

In a moment Trent and Morris came dashing down the bank and onto the raft. Terry untied the rope, but left a turn around the tree till the two men were aboard. Then he dropped the rope and followed them.

They soon gained headway. The river had narrowed and stretched straight away for some distance, which was in favor of the pioneers. The enemy would be busy just keeping up, for the flow of the stream was swifter when the stream was narrow.

Tip sent Jan, Chris, and two of the men to take cover with Trent and Morris behind the stock. "You can't protect them so use them as a shield," he said. "John, Cal, stay in the middle. Lie low behind the pole wall. Norie, Connie, keep down, too, unless you see an Indian in range of your buckshot. The rest of you stay here with me," he said. "Crouch low to make a small target."

"We heard three shots," Jan said to Trent. "Did one of the Shawnees shoot?"

"No," Trent explained, "Morris held his shot a half minute after my first shot. That stopped them long enough so I could reload. My last Indian ducked behind his tree just as I shot. Don't think I got him. Slowed them up, though. Unless they catch up in the next couple of hours, they won't make us any trouble today."

An hour later the river curved to the south. When, some time later, it developed that they were rounding the point of a great curve that circled back to the north, Tip was worried. "If the Shawnees know this river, they will cross this bend and save a lot of distance," he said. "You women better keep down when the river starts to bend back."

They were feeling less anxiety when they had rounded the curve and were floating again on a straightaway to the west. "Guess they didn't make it," Tip said.

He had scarcely finished speaking when a flight of arrows flicked out from the dense undergrowth. The crack of several rifles came with them. One of the horses fell and floundered about on the rear raft, and two arrows quivered in the poles that protected the women. Although he said nothing about it at the time, a bullet cut between the arm and ribs of one of the men— Donlin, by name. The gash across his ribs was not deep.

Trent's rifle was at his shoulder in an instant, and he fired at the bushes. "Might have hit him," he said.

Young Chris Hoffer put his rifle in Trent's hands. "I'll load yours," he said.

Two or three more arrows came from the bushes, but the raft was drifting rapidly away from the ambush, and the arrows did no harm. Trent and Tip were not looking back; they were looking ahead. "I don't believe we heard from all those rifles," Tip said.

The answer came immediately. There was a puff of smoke from the leafy, widespread branches some distance ahead and a scream from the middle raft. Tip's and Trent's rifles

spoke almost as one. With a shaking of the
branches, an Indian fell to the ground, his body
half hanging over the high bank of the stream.
His rifle was sticking deep in the mud near his
trailing hand.

On the spur of the moment, Jan dived off the
raft and swam swiftly to the rifle. But when he
tried to pull it from the mud, it was so well
anchored that he had to come half out of the
water and plant his feet on the shallow, muddy
bottom at the edge of the river in order to wrench
the gun from the clinging mud. As he straightened up, the rifle in his hands, two sinewy red
arms reached out of the foliage. Two strong
hands grasped the long hair on his head and
lifted and threw him back into the edge of the
leafy cover.

Though young and active, Jan's strength fell
far short of matching that of the powerful
Shawnee whose fingers were wound in his hair.
He heard cries from the rafts, but realized that
too much of the action on the bank was hidden
by the leafy foliage to permit a shot that would

save him. Strangely enough, anger at his own rashness, rather than fear, was Jan's reaction to this desperate situation. Instinctively, he seized the Shawnee's wrists as he straightened up to drag his captive back into the forest, threw himself back, and kicked both feet with all his strength into the bare stomach. The unlooked-for attack doubled the Indian over and jerked him forward. The two, with Jan's hands still locked around the red man's thick wrists, dived headfirst into the shallow water with sufficient force to shoot them out into the deeper current.

Jan quickly realized that he was more at home in the water than his stronger adversary, but the Indian, realizing that he would be instantly picked off by the riflemen the moment he rose above the water, stubbornly held on to Jan as a shield. As they momentarily rose to the surface, Jan got a glimpse of the rear raft already fifty feet away down the stream, and the Shawnee was pulling him down again. His only hope was to get far enough from the Indian to permit the riflemen to get in a clear shot. He pointed his

feet toward the bank and started kicking and stroking in a manner that trailed the red man behind him. As they rose to the surface, Jan heard the crack of rifles. The Shawnee's grasp on his hair loosened as the bleeding body floated away on the current.

Jan struck out with all his speed to regain the raft. Somewhere in the rear he heard a shot, and

a bullet zipped near his head. He heard answering shots from the raft as he dived and swam under water till he was forced to come up for a gulp of air. With the current to help him, he gradually overtook the raft, repeating this maneuver. But after the strenuous efforts of the past few minutes, he was near to exhaustion. Then Terry made a cast with the tail rope, which he had held in readiness. Jan gratefully grasped the trailing rope, and Terry reeled him in.

He sat on the edge of the raft a minute to get back his breath and strength before rising. When he turned around the men, at a wave from Tip, were on their way back to their stations. Only Tip and Trent remained, with Terry coiling up the tail rope, and the set of their features was bleak indeed. Tip's face was flushed with anger.

"Never let me see you do a stunt like that again," he said in a tense voice. "We might have had the choice of tying up to make an attempt to rescue you or leaving you to your fate, which wouldn't have been nice to think about, considering the number of braves we've sent to the happy hunting ground. If we had stopped, some of us would have been sure to be killed—not to speak of the women."

Jan glanced at Trent, but Trent had deliberately turned his back. Apparently he agreed with Tip, and there was no friendly smile on the face of any man in sight. The censure seemed to be unanimous.

"It looked easy at the time, Tip," Jan gave as his defense. "I didn't think I would have any trouble getting it."

"Well, don't do a silly trick like that again," Tip answered. Then, relenting a bit, he added, "I suppose you thought you were doing something for the good of the party. We're just lucky that it turned out as it did. Wait for orders the next time one of those quick ideas strikes you."

"Yes, sir," Jan answered. He was seething within, but he realized the justice of Tip's anger.

Considering himself dismissed, he made the long walk down the length of the rafts, looking neither to left or right, except to pause beside his mother, kiss her wet cheek, and whisper, "I'm sorry, Mom." He felt that he had aged ten years in the last ten minutes.

An hour before dark they tied up beside an open, grassy spot on the opposite side from where they had left the Shawnees. "We must be twenty miles beyond the ambush," Trent estimated. "We've floated enough miles to be twice that far. This may not be the crookedest river in the world, but it's sure the kinkiest."

"We'll sleep ashore tonight," Tip said, "but we'll take all precautions." He detailed some of the men to help the girls pull a supply of grass for the stock. "Pull plenty to last all day tomorrow," he ordered. "Better skin that dead horse, too. We can use the meat. Now let's get a fire going. We must take that bullet out of Mrs. Tyndal's leg."

It was Mrs. Harris who diagnosed the wound. "The bullet," she said, "hit high on the thigh and ranged down till it hit the bone. I don't think it's broken. I can feel a bulge where the bullet is lodged."

"Lucky Indians don't usually load as heavily

as we do," Trent said, "or it would have done more damage."

Mrs. Harris swished a sharp hunting knife in a bucket of boiling water before making the incision to extract the lead, while Tyndal and Trent held the wounded woman still.

"Bring me the bandages," she said. "It's a clean wound; I think it will heal nicely. I'll sleep beside you tonight, my dear," she told the young woman, "and take care of you and the baby."

7.

Landing at the Falls

Jan sprang up when he heard Tip and Trent turn out of their blankets two hours before daylight. He accepted Tip's order to rout the company out. "Better have a good breakfast," Tip told the women. "We'll be plenty busy later on. I figure we're pretty close to our destination— just an hour or two on the river. Those Shawnees behind us may catch up sometime today, but we can handle them without much trouble, once we've landed. Another band may be hunting in the vicinity, though."

Their experience of the day before had perfected their loading technique. Heindrich Hoffer carried Mrs. Tyndal aboard as easily as though she were a child and laid her on a bed of blankets over a pad of tips from fir branches. "I'm not used to so much attention," she said with a smile. "I think I'll get shot again sometime."

Tip's timetable was right. The sun was just edging up over the horizon when Tip pointed to the sparsely wooded bank half a mile ahead. "There it is," he said. "We'll tie up after we've drifted a little way around that curve. The river makes a sharp loop there; it's only a scant quarter mile across the point."

There was a trace of excitement on the faces of the entire company, though they had little to say. They were wondering what the coming days, months, or—as they hoped—years might bring forth. They had no illusions as to the magnitude of the struggle necessary to establish and maintain a home here, surrounded by virgin forest and hostile red men.

Terry had his rope ready for the tie-up. Tip asked him, "Are you a good swimmer?"

Terry answered, "No, I don't swim too well."

Then Jan spoke up quickly. "I'll take the rope

ashore, Tip. And why not have Chris and Terry
go ashore, too, off the lead raft to help tie up?"

"Chris, Terry, go down to the lead raft and be
ready to jump when Jan does," Tip ordered.

The river was much broader here than at the
point where they had started the day before.
Creeks entering it had doubled its flow. The
rafts were rounding into the curve, but twenty
feet of water flowed between them and the shore.
It was apparent that the action of the current
would not swing them closer.

"Jump, Jan!" Tip ordered. "Terry, Chris, get
ashore!"

Jan just managed to get his feet on land as he
came to the end of the rope. He ran down the
shore till he met the other two. They dashed up
the bank and twirled the rope around a small
walnut tree—the only suitable tree near enough
to the water. The rafts swung slowly into the
low bank as they took up the slack in the rope.

"Well done, boys," Tip told them. "Now
everybody get busy and unload." Trent, Morris,
and two more men stepped ashore and fanned

out through the trees. A short distance from the riverbank the timber stood thick over the entire surface of the loop. It would be a good place to defend.

A faint rumbling sound was in the air, seemingly coming from down the river. "What's that strange noise, Tip?" one of the women asked.

"That's the roar of the falls," Tip replied. "It's just a little way below the opposite side of this loop. If the boys hadn't made a good job of snubbing these rafts to a tree, we'd be taking a trip over them about now."

Terry came dashing down the bank. To the few still on the lead raft, he cried, "Get off! Get off! The tree is starting to pull loose!"

"Get the rest of the women off that middle raft," he yelled at the men on the bank. He brought down his woodsman's ax across the rope which linked the two together. The lead raft floated away as he sprang ashore. With a third of the pull removed, the walnut anchor tree would hold.

Tip had observed the few moments of fast

action by Terry. "Quick thinking, Terry," he complimented the young man. "You've paid your way on this trip."

The men who had leaped from the raft turned to watch it swing out on its way to plunge over the falls. Two shots rang out from some distance back in the timber. There was a flat *spatt*. Grandpa Clem bent down and picked up a piece of flattened lead that had been a bullet when it struck the anvil. "You carry good armor, Heindrich," he said.

Tip snatched his rifle and slipped into the timber just as two more shots were heard. In a short time he was back, carrying an extra rifle. "Those two shots came from a bunch of half a dozen Indians, Trent tells me," he reported. "The last two shots accounted for one of them. The others were leaving fast. Now let's get busy with our axes and saws. We'll cut trees enough to string across this loop as a barricade to protect us from the land side. Get the horses harnessed. We have a long day before us."

The entire party threw every effort into making their fortifications. Tyndal's horses were well-trained and a great help in swinging sections of tree trunks in place. By nightfall logs and whole tree trunks had been strung together so that they reached from one side of the loop to the other. The barricade arched in toward the center a little, so the defenders could see any portion of it from their station behind it. The logs had been stacked two high—in some places higher. The men cut the trees and underbrush from the area in front and threw everything into piles. "We'll burn these heaps after dark," Tip said, "so the smoke won't be seen. That bunch that was here today will soon spread the word, though, and the band that was following us knows we had to stop above the falls."

The few Indians who had fired on them in the morning had not been heard from again. "Probably a small band of hunters," Tip figured. "The band we met up the river may have given up for the time being. But they'll be back. You can bank on that, and there will be more with them."

The rafts were cut loose. Terry carefully

chopped out all the nails he could salvage and took off the chain and rope before they were released. Some of the party watched as the rafts swung out into the river and rode to take the plunge, with a feeling bordering on affection. They had served their passengers well. Their use had no doubt saved some lives.

In the next weeks everyone in the party threw himself into the project of building homes and planting the seed, carried so many weary miles. They would be able to eat only a portion of the fruits of their plantings. Seed for the following spring must be saved.

It was mostly the women who prepared the land and planted the seed, which would flourish in the rich soil. Wooden handles were fashioned for the hoes, which had been carried from Boonsboro. Burdick's plow was assembled and used to break up the newly cleared land.

Until a full crop was raised, food would be a major problem. Twelve-year-old Hughie Donlin and Donald MacGregor, a year younger, spent much of the time catching fish from the river. They were plentiful, and the boys used strong lines. And when, as frequently happened, they hooked into a giant catfish, they both hung onto the pole while they screamed for help from the grownups. Trent, Ed Thomas with his bow, and usually two other companions made forays into the forest for deer, elk, bear, and buffalo. It was figured that four men would run a good chance of fighting their way back, should they run into trouble. If no game was approached close enough for a bow shot, a rifle shot was risked. Guns had to be used on buffalo too, for they were seldom killed by an arrow only. Jan's desire to shoot elk and buffalo was satisfied.

A couple of low pens, built of poles in the manner of a log house and covered with brush, were maintained as turkey traps. A narrow trench slanted down under the wall of the pen and then slanted up. The usually wary birds would pick at the bait on the trench bottom, and move up into the enclosure. Then with heads high they would try to escape through the narrow spaces between the poles. They never looked down at the trench again. Gobblers wandered in small flocks after the mating season, and frequently several ended up in a trap.

Watercress was found in a small creek nearby, and other greens abounded in the woods. They were gathered under the guard of several rifles, for no one except Trent or Tip was permitted to leave the camp alone. Trent went on scouting trips deep into the forest, now and then, slipping away before daylight and returning only after dark. He was expert in covering his trail, and read the signs of the forest as well as the Indians, whose trails he sought. Jan was thrilled when Trent once took him on an all-day scout. He sensed his liking for him, though Trent never expressed himself. And Jan's respect for him was steadily increasing.

8.
The
New
Settlement

The first days of September saw many changes on the forty-acre plot of land within the bend of the river. Some twenty acres of land had been hastily cleared. The small trees had been cut, the trunks saved for house building, and the trimmings and small brush burned. The big trees had been girdled. A shallow notch, chopped entirely around the trunks, killed the trees, and permitted the sun to shine through the branches. In three or four years the hardwood stumps would rot out, and the field would be clear. Every member of the party had worked to the limit of his endurance, for only by much effort and ceaseless vigilance could they hope to secure safety.

Then one Sunday everyone except the sentinels took a whole day off for the first festive occasion. Some of the women helped Jan's mother decorate her cabin with big bunches of wild flowers and cedar boughs. Mrs. Thomas found enough white flour left in camp to make a big cake, using wild honey to sweeten it. Mrs. Hoffer contributed the last half pound of her precious coffee, and Mr. Hoffer smashed the beans up on his anvil, since there was no grinder.

Unanimous opinion was that the first wedding in the colony rated a complete holiday. Terry and Katie had been engaged a year, and there was no reason why they shouldn't marry. Terry was nineteen and youthful marriages were the rule among the pioneers. Too often life was short and loaded with responsibility that men never knew in a more protected society.

There was little in the appearance of the members of the company to indicate that this day was different from any other, except that everybody appeared scrubbed, shaved, and with hair carefully combed. The women wore their best gingham dresses. The men still wore the buckskin shirts with which they had started the trek into this hostile no-man's land.

When the signal was given, Howard Tyndal played, on the violin he had included in his small pack as a necessity, a lilting march as Katie and Terry marched out of the cabin to the cleared space in front, where the entire company, except the sentinels, was gathered.

Mrs. Williams, who had heard the marriage rites said many times by her Presbyterian father and was recognized as the religious leader of the group, repeated the lines from memory. She concluded with the time-honored words, "Kiss the bride," always added to convince the dazed groom that he was now a married man.

Congratulations were expressed. Both Molly Harris and Cora Seaton shed the few tears tradition demanded. The buckskin-shirted woodsmen kissed the bride, and the women kissed the groom.

Katie cut the wedding cake with her hus-

band's hunting knife, which had been thoroughly cleaned for the purpose, and everyone sat
down to the line of homemade tables heaped
with a plentiful supply of the best the camp afforded: fish, turkey, and elk, with green vegetables from the spring planting.

After the wedding dinner, a space on the hard-beaten ground was cleared for a square dance in full swing to the tune of Howard's fiddle. Doyle Donlin was doing the calling, the singsong cadence of his voice rising and falling with the music. Colin MacGregor beat time on a drum he had made by stretching a tanned coonskin over a section of hollow gum tree. Even Tip and Trent, who were alternating on sentry duty, danced with Molly Harris and Linnette Tyndal, whose injured leg had completely healed. The small fry danced and played about in high glee.

After two hours of this, the work-hardened dancers were still going strong, when three shots rang out from the woods across the clearing. Two bullets smacked into the logs of the cabin behind the dancers. The men snatched up their rifles, leaning conveniently against the cabins.

"Everybody in the cabins," Tip ordered.

There was no more shooting. When, an hour later, Trent crawled in from his station behind the log barricade, he passed the opinion that there would be no attack. "Lay low till dusk, and we'll see what happens."

"Four men will stay on guard tonight," Tip decided. "We'll do some investigating in the morning."

An hour before daylight Trent, Morris, Tyndal, and Jan stole down to the river, and followed along the bank till they were well into the forest. An hour after daylight they returned across the clearing. "The signs showed there were only three Indians," Trent said. "They've pulled out. We can go to work, but we had better keep a close watch."

In the warm September sun the corn ripened, was cut, and set up in shocks to season. Later the ears would be husked out, and the fodder would be fed to the cattle and horses. Enough seed had been carried along to seed an acre of mixed clover and timothy for horse feed.

Most of the harvesting was done by the women, for the men were already engaged in building the blockhouse, so necessary for their protection from the marauding Shawnees. Their great hope was that it would be finished before a big force might gather to attack them.

"Most attacks come in the spring or summer," Trent said one evening at a meeting of the elders. "Usually the Shawnees stay close to their villages north of the Ohio during the winter season, though winters are frequently mild this far south. We had better have this fort finished and the clearing extended by the time the buds start to burst. We can't afford to ease up."

Tip agreed with this analysis of their situation. "A lot of settlers have come into this section south of the Ohio the past year," he said. "Two settlements are due to be made between ours and Harrodsburg in the spring, and there will be more. If we can hold this place through another summer, we'll be pretty safe."

The cabins for each family had been built tight together and in a straight row, facing the forest, so that they would be easy to defend. When finished, the blockhouse would rise above them. A twenty-foot space was left in the middle of the cabin row, so a sort of ell of the blockhouse could be built between and beyond the cabins. Building a structure large enough to over-shadow the line of cabins was a heavy project for a handful of men, some of whom had to be al-ways on guard. The blockhouse had to be over a hundred feet long and two stories high, with the upper story projecting out over the walls of the lower story, so any attackers reaching the walls could be seen through the projecting floor above. Portholes looked out all around the upper story, so that all the approaches to the blockhouse could be watched. The middle section of the fort was built complete before the wings were con-tinued each way from the center. The end walls would become partitions when the wings were extended.

"The lower rooms will make a safe place for the stock and some feed," Tip figured.

With Grandpa Clem supervising, the men dug a well forty feet deep inside the blockhouse. They had to go down that far, because the settle-ment was on a rise, but they ended up with four feet of water in the well. Grandpa Clem hewed out and notched locust cribbing, and they cribbed the well from top to bottom.

A five-foot runway was left between the rear of the cabins and the lower wall of the blockhouse. Access to any part of the buildings could be gained from this corridor. The cabins had been roofed with shakes split from straight-grained blocks of pine and cedar, but the blockhouse was roofed with long, overlapping slabs, hewed out by expert men. "They won't catch fire so easily," Terry said.

Little time could be wasted for socializing, but it became a custom to dance two or three hours on Saturday nights. Sunday mornings the company gathered to hear Mrs. Williams read a chapter from the Bible and make a short talk. They all enjoyed the singing at these meetings. But at the conclusion of the hour of worship they again took up their work.

As the smaller logs were brought in from the forest, the larger trees up to a hundred yards from the buildings were also cut. This removed close cover for attackers and cleared the land for crops. Tree trunks of great diameter were rolled together and kept burning till they were reduced to ashes. Trunks under two feet in diameter were cut into lengths and stood in a solid line, the lower end buried three feet in the ground, to form a circular stockade eight feet high around the buildings.

This was hard, grueling work, but the little company stuck doggedly to its task, alert to the danger of being completely wiped out if it did not provide adequate fortifications. When the warm March sun had melted the last of the snow, the stockade and the sturdy walls of the blockhouse were in place and the roof was half finished.

9.

The Gobbler Called

The fort had been finished for several weeks, and summer had advanced to the early days of July. Jan, sitting in the shadow of the blockhouse, passed an old shirtsleeve, moistened with bear oil, lovingly over the metal and walnut stock of the rifle he had inherited from his father.

The sun was two hours high, and he knew he should be thinking of work in the fields instead of listening to the occasional gobble of a turkey on the bluffs along the river. But it seemed that, as had been the case with his father, his hands were better fitted to grasp a rifle than the handle of a hoe or ax. He looked reflectively across the clearing that surrounded the fort as the gobble,

gobble, gobble of the turkey came again clearly upon the morning breeze.

Orderly rows of corn, beans, and potatoes marched out across that part of the clearing which lay closest to the fort. But between these crops and the encircling forest, patches of wheat and meadows of timothy and clover took up the space. These low-growing crops did not lend themselves well to cover a creeping foe. They would be harvested under the eyes of vigilant sentinels, whose warning would cause the workers to snatch up rifles near at hand.

Heindrich Hoffer paused on his way to the fields. "You spend more time polishing that gun, Jan, than you do working," he said.

"Don't you keep your rifle in good condition, Mr. Hoffer?" Jan asked, not too much nettled by a statement carrying so much truth.

"You know, Jan, that I have no rifle," the big man replied. "Just a shotgun."

But before passing on his way, he gave Jan a pat on his shoulder. "I guess it is well that some can shoot so others may work," he said.

Jan smiled and went back to checking the number of bullets in his pouch. In a few minutes Doyle Donlin came by. "Seen Trent around this morning?" he inquired. He knew that Trent always left word, often with Jan, before starting on one of his scouting trips.

"Left before daylight, as usual," Jan told Donlin. "You know he always gets away early so any Indian lurking around won't see him leave. Got something for him?" He noticed that Donlin was carrying a loaf of bread.

"Yes, the wife said to give him this," Donlin said. "These women worry more about Trent than they do about their hard-working husbands." But there was no malice in his voice.

"Give it to me. I'm going over to his cabin in a minute," Jan said. His mother had already asked Jan to take over a bowl of venison stew, flavored with plenty of onions and other vegetables. Everyone concerned himself with keeping Trent's larder well supplied. That he spent much of his time in the woods was much to the settlement's benefit.

Jan tucked the loaf of bread under his arm and made his way to the small room in one end of the blockhouse, which Trent referred to as his cabin. The fact that he was carrying a rifle aroused no curiosity from those he met. He was seldom seen without it.

After he left the food in Trent's room, Jan closed the door and stood for a moment on the bank of the little creek that flowed through the stockade and by Trent's door on its way out of the clearing. The call of the gobbler on the bluff came again to his ear. The temptation proved too strong to resist. He stepped down into the creek; the water came only halfway to his knees. The banks from this point to the woods were quite high, and tall grass grew along the top edges. By stooping, he was hidden from the sight of anyone who might glance in his direction. "I'll cut this grass when I get back," he muttered. "If I can keep out of sight on the way out, Indians can do the same on the way in."

He continued on his way, and left the creek only when he had penetrated far enough into the forest to be well out of sight of anyone in the clearing. He looked back at the blockhouse, with its upper story jutting out over the walls of the lower story. Apparently he had been unobserved.

I'll be back in an hour, he resolved. With Trent away, his absence would go unnoticed.

Jan struck away up the river in the direction of the gobbler's call. It was repeated at long intervals. "I'll have to hurry," he told himself. "It may quit for the day."

Nevertheless, he proceeded with the caution his father had taught him through years in the woods. His moccasins silently trod the carpet of leaves on the forest floor. He stopped frequently, when hidden in some clump of brush, to glance keenly in all directions and to listen for any sound in the forest, such as the disturbed scolding from the birds and small red pine squirrels that were always resentful of intrusion.

As he neared the source of the calls, his approach became even more cautious. He carefully scanned the ground ahead each time he set down a foot. The rustle of the leaves or the snap of a twig would betray his presence to the gobbler, for nothing has keener sight or hearing than a wild turkey. He moved only a short distance after hearing the last call, and waited patiently till the next call was given. Deciding that the gobbler was around the corner of the bluff, he moved some distance to the right. This, he figured, would give him a clear line of vision except for the brush. When the next call came, quite close now, he started again to finish his stalk of the alert game.

Jan hadn't moved a yard when the report of a rifle rang out from the top of the bluff. Since he heard no beating wings of a turkey in flight, he assumed, with a touch of disgust, that some hunter had beaten him to the kill. His natural caution, however, warned him to stay concealed until he found out who the hunter might be.

Soon he was enlightened. "You can come out now, Jan," Trent called, as he looked over the rocky edge of the bluff.

Jan's face betrayed his embarrassment at being caught out of bounds, as well as disappointment at having lost an opportunity to bag a gobbler.

"You said you were going up to the gap today," Jan said, with a challenge in his voice. He felt he must say something to save his face.

"Still am—later," Trent agreed. He came down off the high rock and sat on the trunk of a fallen tree. "We can keep an eye up through the woods from here," he said.

The lecture Jan knew he deserved was milder than he expected. "You were given as good training as any boy in this wild country, Jan," Trent told him. "Your father never would have come out as openly as you did today, just for the sake of shooting a turkey. Besides, you broke the rule of the settlement, that nobody leaves the place without letting it be known. If you never came back, who would know what had become of you? Your mother has had enough loss for one woman."

"There haven't been any Indians around here for weeks," Jan offered in halfhearted defense.

"Besides, I came out down the creek, hidden all the way."

"From up here," Trent replied, dryly, "you were anything but hidden. I saw you all the way. An Indian could have done the same. Better pick up your turkey," he concluded, "and get back home. I'll be on my way."

Jan rose, without much enthusiasm, to collect the game Trent had robbed him of an opportunity to shoot, after his careful stalk. He made his way around the corner of the bluff to the point where he had last heard the gobbler and clambered over a big rock. He looked down, and there, instead of the gobbler he had expected to see, lay a dead Indian, with streaks of war paint across his face—a mere boy perhaps a year or two older than himself. Though Indians had been his enemy as long as he could remember, his feelings were more pity than hatred for this boy who had started from his village in high hopes of returning with the scalp of a white man as evidence that he had proved himself a warrior, worthy to be received as an equal with the older braves at the council fire.

Jan did not delude himself. Had Trent not lingered in the vicinity, his own scalp might have been the young brave's trophy. Crestfallen, he returned to his seat on the fallen tree. He felt very inadequate and humble, but couldn't find the words to say so. His opinion of Trent rose even more when the scout remarked, as though nothing unusual had happened, "Guess I'd better be on my way up the country. I'll be back by dark. Want to find out whether a whole party has come this way, or just this boy. You might remember," he added, "that the mating season for turkeys is long past. Think that over next time you hear a gobbler calling in July."

"I'll remember, Trent," Jan answered. "I should have thought of that." Then he added, in a voice filled with curiosity, "You didn't take his scalp, Trent."

"Never do," Trent replied shortly. "Why humiliate a dead man? After all, this is their country. They fight for what is really their own.

We have to shoot Indians, Jan, but we don't have to hate them." He rose without further words, and walked swiftly away up an aisle through the trees.

Puzzled, Jan watched Trent as he swung away with unhurried, distance-eating strides. He had never heard the usually taciturn woodsman express himself so frankly. He had always assumed that Trent must hate the Indians as they, no doubt, hated the invaders of their primeval forests.

Jan rose to leave. A few steps more and Trent would be out of sight among the trees. He glanced at Trent one last time and was galvanized into instinctive action. A painted Indian, with feathers stuck in his scalp lock, had stepped from a small beech thicket. As he raised his rifle, Jan threw his own rifle to his shoulder and trained the sights on the broad back. At the crack of the rifle, the warrior slumped in his tracks.

Trent whirled and threw himself prone, his rifle at his shoulder. After cautiously examining every inch of the surrounding forest, he came back down through the trees, being careful this time to keep under cover. He picked up the rifle of the fallen brave. Jan had just finished reloading when Trent joined him.

With his eyes still roving over the surrounding forest, Trent sat down again on the tree trunk. His voice carried a distinct note of respect when he said, "We seem to be taking turns at lifesaving today, Jan. That big warrior couldn't have missed me at this distance. When did you first see him?"

"He stepped out just as I was getting up to

leave," Jan told him. "He was raising his gun. I
shot first and thought afterward, I guess."

"A quick shot and a long shot," Trent

summed it up. "I think you'll do to take along."

Jan flushed self-consciously at the high praise.
A compliment from these backwoods people was
usually well earned. He bypassed the whole
matter by saying, "Guess I'd better be getting
back to the fort. I'll take in the two rifles."

"Go back a different way," Trent cautioned
him. "If other Indians are around, they'll expect
you to return by the same route. Haven't found
much sign here except what was made by that
one boy, but I'll do some looking around before
starting up to the gap."

"You'll be putting in a hard day, Trent," Jan
said. "Suppose you come over for supper when
you get back."

"Be glad to," Trent replied. "Probably be
about dark if I don't run into trouble."

Heeding Trent's advice, Jan struck deeper into
the wood and proceeded in a roundabout way to
the point where the creek left the clearing. He
lay in a thicket many minutes, watching for any
indication of a hidden enemy, before starting up
the creek.

His inclination was all for going out to work with the men in the fields without mentioning to anyone where he had been or what had taken place, but he decided it was only right that Tip should know.

Tip looked him over coldly. "I suppose you realize you've broken a hard and fast rule that nobody, except Trent, leaves this clearing unless ordered to," he said. "If everybody starts making his own rules, we won't last long. We'd be picked off one at a time, just as you would have been if Trent hadn't been around to take care of you. Now, since you're available for duty again, go keep an eye on the west side of the clearing. I'll put Morris on the other side, and Norie is standing guard on the river side."

"I'll stop in a minute to speak to Mother," Jan told Tip. "Then I'll be right out."

Mrs. Harris didn't reproach her son when he related the events of the morning. Perhaps she figured that a rebuke from both Trent and Tip was enough. Jan paused a moment at the door. "Trent will be here for supper tonight."

"Good," she answered. "I'll stew some dried sweet corn and bake a pie."

As Jan hurried to take up the post Tip had assigned him, he thought of the little smile that had lighted her face.

10.
Saturday
Night
Supper

Tip did not come to relieve Jan till well after dark. "Trent is in," he said. "He reports signs of Indians moving around up toward the river, but none within miles of here. You two got 'em all this morning, it seems. You may as well go in." His manner was still far from cordial.

Jan answered pleasantly and turned toward home. He found his mother preparing supper, and noticed that the single big room of the log cabin was all cleaned and tidied up. Mrs. Harris was wearing her best flowered gingham dress, with the high lace collar, and it became her.

"Everyone seems to know about your hunt this morning," she said to Jan. "I suppose Tip told them. You aren't very popular just now.

Don't lose your temper if you're criticized.
You've provoked it, you know."

Trent's knock at the door ended the conversation, to Jan's relief. At his call of, "Come in,"
Trent pulled the latchstring of the heavy door

and entered. His long hair was combed smooth-
ly, and he had taken time to shave above his
mustache and short beard.

"Good evening, Mrs. Harris," Trent re-
sponded to Jan's mother's greeting. During all
the years he had known her, he had never called
her Molly, even though he had been a close
friend and companion of her husband.

Never a great talker, Trent left most of the
conversation at the table to Jan and his mother,
though he complimented her upon the meal,
especially the stewed sweet corn. "Only corn
I've had since last season," he said.

"I want to dry much more," Mrs. Harris said.
"The new corn will soon be ready to pick. Too
bad we don't have milk to cook it in."

After the pie was disposed of, Trent and Jan
sat back and talked while Mrs. Harris cleared
the table. She carried the red-checked cloth to
the door and shook out the crumbs, as she stood
on the split-log stoop. Then pouring water from
the steaming teakettle and adding a dash of soft
soap, she washed the dishes.

"I'll throw out the dish water, Mom," Jan offered. He picked up the nicely hollowed-out wooden trough, and carried it out of doors.

When Mrs. Harris had seated herself in the plain, but comfortable rocker Terry had made her, she picked up a shirt of the usual buckskin and started working on it. "I can scarcely keep up with him," she remarked.

After a moment's silence, Trent brought up something he had on his mind. "I should make a trip up to Fort Nelson in Louisville," he said, "if things stay quiet here till fall. I'd like to find out more about what the Indian situation really is. Would you consent to Jan's going along? It would be good experience for him. Besides, it would be safer for two traveling through a hostile country."

Jan was surprised at this last statement. Trent was practically putting him on the footing of an experienced and competent woodsman.

Trent continued. "This General Clark at Fort Nelson is a real Indian fighter. I want to meet him. Maybe I'll go up and join him later. He needs experienced scouts. There'll be plenty of excitement up there for a long time."

Jan glanced at his mother. She quietly laid the shirt she was stitching on the table. Two bright spots were smoldering in her cheeks, and there was an angry gleam in her dark brown eyes. Her voice, though tense, was well controlled when she spoke. "You men," she began, "are all of one mold. When matters get settled and normal, you move on someplace where you can find trouble and hardship. Tom was the same. After Jan was born, he moved us to the western part of Virginia, where the Cherokees were still raiding the settlements. Three moves and a dozen years later we were still following in the wake of Indian troubles. But when we came here, we overtook them."

Both Trent and Jan followed her words with startled attention. Jan had never seen his mother so agitated before.

"Is it your ambition, Trent," she asked, "to finally die all by yourself in a lonely trapper's shack?" She settled back in her rocker, stripped a length of the strong linen thread off the spool, and started to thread her needle. "I know," she resumed more quietly, "that what you do is none of my business. And I do wish to thank you for taking care of Jan this morning."

"I haven't gone yet," Trent said. "Don't get so stirred up about it—Molly." A slow smile showed in his eyes at her startled look.

That seemed to end the conversation, and later on Jan left to play checkers with Chris Hoffer, as he did every Saturday night. From the path he trod, he could see the blockhouse, outlined clearly by the light of a new moon, just rising above the treetops. He paused a moment to look off across a field of waving corn, viewing the beauty of the still summer night with all the satisfaction of one born and reared close to nature. Jan had come to love this place.

11.

The Shawnees Gather

The next few days were not spent too happily by Jan. The episode of the turkey hunt had made a most unfavorable impression on all the members of the little settlement. But Jan remembered his mother's warning about not losing his temper, and swallowed his discomfiture when the matter was brought up.

Mrs. MacGregor, always outspoken, especially took him to task. " 'Tis a stubborn will you have, laddie," she told him, when he happened to meet her on his way to work. "Better that you should listen to your elders than to go gallivanting alone in the woods." Relenting a bit, she added, "So good a shot as yourself we canna afford to lose. We need all the strong arms and sharp eyes in this lonely wilderness filled with savages and hardship."

"Yes, Mrs. MacGregor, you're quite right," Jan answered politely, though his face was flushed with resentment.

His resentment was even greater when Chris twitted him about his unfavorable rating in the community. Though the two boys seemed friendly enough on the surface, an underlying tinge of rivalry sometimes showed through. Chris, several years older than Jan, resented Jan's superior marksmanship, though he was far from being a bad rifleman himself.

Chris had forborne to mention the turkey hunt when Jan had come as a guest to play checkers, but the next day, when they were working in the field, he couldn't resist bringing it up. "Guess Tip laid you out pretty well for chasing off after a turkey, huh? How does it seem not to have everyone patting you on the back?"

"My back can get along without the patting— just as yours does," Jan answered shortly. Then, remembering his mother's warning, he moved over to another part of the field, seething with anger.

It was Norie's words of sympathy that restored his equanimity. She joined him after supper as he was making good his commitment to cut the rank grass at the top of the high banks of the creek, under the watchful eye of two sentinels. He was using his hunting knife as a sickle, moving his rifle along as he worked.

"I wanted to tell you, Jan," Norie said, keeping a sharp eye on the forest, "that I don't think folks are fair, treating you the way they have. I told Mother and Dad they should give you credit for saving Trent's life, instead of just blaming you for breaking a rule."

Jan sat back on his heels and looked up at Norie. "It's good to hear someone taking my part," he said. "But to be honest about the whole thing, Trent probably wouldn't have been caught off guard if I hadn't been on his mind. I can't take credit. Everyone will forget it soon.

There isn't much to talk about here, with all of us cooped up together."

Trent was waiting at the end of the blockhouse when Jan finished trimming the grass back to where the little creek came close to the buildings. He told Jan, "I'm going out again before daylight, and I want you to go along. I didn't much like finding so many Indian signs up around the gap. I've checked with Tip, so he'll know where you are. Better go home and get some sleep. You'll need to be fresh for a hard day's travel."

On his way to the cabin, Jan wondered whether this was Trent's way of expressing his disapproval of the treatment Jan had received or whether Trent had something of greater importance in mind. His mother, Jan found, had also seen Trent and was disturbed at his intimation that the settlement might be in real danger of an attack. "I believe you're safe with Trent anywhere," she told Jan. "I suppose everybody must do his part, but I want both of you to come back."

Jan was sleeping with the carefree mind of youth when his mother awakened him next morning. She had insisted that Trent should share their breakfast, and she also gave them some meat and corn bread, wrapped in a rhubarb leaf. Usually a pouch of parched corn was all a scout carried.

After she had given Jan a hug, with the time-honored admonition to "be careful," they made their way down to the river and stole noiselessly along the bank. A mile above the settlement, they dragged out a pirogue, a canoe made by hollowing out a log, from where it was well hidden and crossed the river. When the first streaks of day appeared, Trent struck northward, staying as much as possible under cover. Where the trees stood clear of all underbrush, he traveled on the side of a ridge, pausing frequently to listen or to peep over the top to scan the woods on the other side. He seldom spoke and, in the interest of speed, was not taking a great deal of pains to hide his tracks.

Two hours away from the settlement, they cut

the trail of two men. After following them a little distance, Trent said, "These tracks are two or three days old. Could have been made by the two we shot."

"One was heavier than the other," Jan observed.

"That's right," Trent agreed.

In another three hours, they came upon the trail of a sizable number of Indians. After studying the tracks on the leaf-carpeted floor of the forest, Trent asked, "How many?"

"I would say more than fifteen," Jan answered.

"Probably more than twenty," Trent decided, "and they are not traveling in the direction of the settlement unless they swing south. They may have passed only a few minutes ago. Some of these plants haven't straightened up yet. We'll follow them a ways to see if they keep to this southwest direction."

Trent set a rapid pace. "Not any danger of an ambush," he said. "They have no reason to believe they are being followed."

His analysis was correct. Half an hour later the
sound of voices came faintly to their ears. They
crept to the top of a hill and looked down on the
Indians they had been trailing. Preparations for
a meal were being made. A buck strung up on a
tree was being skinned. Fires had been lighted.
Then one of the party held up his hand and

spoke, and they all turned to face the north in a listening attitude. Soon another group came in sight. Apparently they had been expected, for they were received with friendly greetings.

Trent counted them as they filed into the opening. "Twenty-five more," he whispered.

They silently backed away from the hill. At a safe distance, they stopped to talk. "These bands have arranged to come together," Trent said. "They wouldn't be wearing war paint if they were a hunting party, and there wouldn't be so many in one group. I'm certain our settlement is to be attacked."

Jan remained silent while Trent thought the matter over carefully. There was urgency, as well as decision, in his voice when he spoke again. "If fifty Shawnees hit our settlement without warning, our people will be wiped out to the last man, woman, and child. Now listen carefully. Circle back a mile, then strike straight for home. Keep an eye out ahead, but make speed. There are probably no Indians between here and the settlement. This party seems to be in no hurry. My guess is that they'll move on after eating and attack in the morning. I'm hoping no more will join them. Tip will know what should be done if he has a little time.

"I won't be going with you. I'll try to get help from Clark at Fort Nelson. The Ohio is only an hour from here at the nearest point. This last bunch no doubt came down the river to that point and hid their canoes to use on their return. If so, I'll find them and destroy all but one, which I'll paddle up the river to Louisville. I won't get there before morning—at the earliest. If Clark will send men in canoes, they can come down the river before the end of the day. Hold these Shawnees off all day tomorrow and the next morning, and we may relieve you in time. Now go and do the best you can."

He put his hand on Jan's shoulder a moment, and added, "You're the nearest to a son that I've ever had. See to it that you and your mother are still there when I get back." He set off at a swift pace, without looking back.

When Jan had left the Shawnee camp well behind, he increased his speed to a jog, tirelessly eating up the miles, though he kept a sharp eye out ahead. He must get home without delay, he kept telling himself, even though he was courting danger by not proceeding with more caution. He struck the river half a mile above the spot where the pirogue was hidden, and he was pleased with his calculation since he had never been on that side of the river before. After paddling across the river, he started on the last mile. He had covered half the distance, when two shots off to one side stopped him. A bullet had cut through the sleeve of his buckskin shirt. Springing behind a tree, he looked in the direction the shots had come from, but could see no movement. If there were only two of the foe, he would make a mistake in giving them a chance to reload. He must take a chance that there were only two Indians. He started running for the clearing.

The two Indians broke from cover, running diagonally in an attempt to cut him off. Jan made a quick stop, threw up his rifle, and shot the lead Indian. Dead tired from the many miles he had traveled, he plucked his woodsman's ax from his belt as he ran. At least, he was as well armed as the Shawnee, who had only a knife and tomahawk.

Suddenly a shot rang out from the forest ahead of Jan. A quick look over his shoulder told him the Shawnee had dropped in his tracks. A moment later he met Tip and Tyndal, who had snatched up their rifles and run to the woods.

"We thought it must be you and Trent," Tip said, as they crossed the clearing. "Where's Trent?"

Jan quickly told him what he and Trent had seen and that Trent had started for Louisville to ask for help. He repeated everything to the other men, who had gathered with rifles in hand to hear what the shooting was about.

Tip issued terse orders. "Donlin, Tyndal, take half the women and start dipping water from the creek to wet the roofs. The first thing Indians do is to set fire to the roofs with flaming arrows. Wet them good. The rest of you women and kids get the stock inside and carry in plenty of feed.

Morris, you and Terry check all the extra rifles. Clean up the two we just brought in. See that they are all loaded and primed. The other men can start cutting the corn nearest the stockade. We'll take a chance on leaving part of it out in the middle of the clearing."

The place was soon a scene of concerted action. Tip's orders were carried out efficiently, yet with all possible speed. As buckets, made for just such an emergency, were passed up a long ladder, Donlin and Tyndal received them and poured the water along the roofs, till the slabs would absorb no more. The shakes on the roofs of the cabins, which sloped back toward the blockhouse, were treated in a similar manner. Several filled buckets were left on the roofs.

Long before dark all of Tip's orders had been attended to. "Probably Trent was right," he said. "The Shawnees may attack during the night, but they are more apt to wait till daybreak. Better get some sleep, Jan. I'll want you on the morning watch."

12.
The
Shawnees
Attack

The thirty-mile jaunt, plus the work to prepare for trouble, had left Jan badly in need of
rest. But danger was on his subconscious mind,
and he awakened instantly at Tip's knock on the
door, completely refreshed.

"Have you time to come in for breakfast,
Tip?" Mrs. Harris called. "It's all ready."

"I'll take another look around and be back in
a few minutes," Tip answered.

"I feel guilty, sleeping half the night, when I
think of Trent," Jan said, as his mother brought
breakfast from the fireplace. "He thought he'd
make it to Fort Nelson by daylight, if he didn't
run into Shawnees on the river. That's a terrible
distance to paddle a canoe without rest."

133

"If anyone can do it, Trent can," Tip said, as he came in.

He repeated the general instructions to Jan's mother, as he and Jan left by the back door into the corridor between the blockhouse and the cabins. "Remember, Mrs. Harris, if any shooting starts, leave the front door barred, and come to the upper floor of the blockhouse. All the women have been told the same."

More of the men were coming up into the blockhouse when Tip and Jan climbed the ladder. "The men who have been here since midnight go down and get your breakfast," Tip ordered. "It may be the last hot meal you'll get for a while." He stationed the relief members at the portholes, which commanded any approach to the fort.

Everything was in order. The upper story of the blockhouse was divided into three rooms, and a long table was set in the middle of each one. On them the men laid out the extra rifles taken in their clashes with the Indians, along with cans of powder and bullets. "Two men must be stationed in the ell beyond the cabins," Tip decided. "But this middle room will need less men than the end rooms, and the small children and some of the women will stay here."

The first streaks of light began to light up the clearing dimly, but no sign of the enemy was evident to the watchful eyes at the portholes. All the men were now in the blockhouse. A few minutes later the entire clearing was visible.

"Perhaps it was a false alarm," Donlin said hopefully. "That band may have been headed west."

"I wish I could believe that," Tip said, "but just because we've seen no Indians doesn't mean that they aren't around. That cornfield may be full of them."

He had scarcely stopped speaking when the place came alive with Indians. Shots from the cornfield were aimed at the portholes to cover other painted Shawnees being boosted by their comrades to the top of the stockade. The rifles of the defenders barked all along the front of the blockhouse. Two of the Shawnees dropped back off the stockade, either killed or wounded. One of the two that had dropped inside was shot down, and the other sprang up and swung back over the top. They had found the settlers prepared.

The women and children poured from the corridor into the blockhouse and climbed to the upper story. Norie and Connie had come up earlier. They were reloading the rifles, so the men could snatch a loaded rifle off the table and return to their stations at once. Mrs. Harris, Mrs. Donlin, and Mrs. Seaton began reloading too.

After the first attempt to reach the fort had ended so disastrously, the Shawnees contented themselves with desultory firing from the woods and cornfield. Their attempts to hit the portholes were seldom successful. Though most of the Indians carried rifles obtained from their French allies, the skill of their shooting did not approach that of the pioneers.

Tip made a check of his forces. He told his men, "We have all the advantage, if they don't manage to set us on fire. That's our greatest danger, for they'll be sure to try it."

His prophecy was proved well founded. Late in the afternoon the Shawnees began shooting flaming arrows from behind the stockade. Some of the arrows fell short and some overshot their target, for the bowmen were handicapped. If they backed off far enough to get a view of the blockhouse, they were exposed to the marksmen at the portholes. Several arrows fell on the roofs, but failed to ignite the wet slabs and shakes.

"With this hot sun," Tip said, "these roofs will be dried out by another day, so some of their arrows may start a blaze. Then we'll be in real trouble."

Night approached, and the Shawnees showed no inclination to push the attack. "They may have decided to wear us down with less loss to themselves," Donlin gave as his opinion. "They have no way of knowing that Trent went for help before they were even here. They probably figure that this siege could last for days with no word of it getting out."

Occasional shots were taken at the fort, but did no damage, for no lights were shown. A couple of candles, set on the floor of each room, were the only illumination. Fire arrows were shot now and then. A fire on a cabin roof was put out before it got well started. Firefighters were little exposed on the cabin roofs, since they sloped back toward the blockhouse. There was no moon, but the night was clear, and the dim light from the stars showed up any skulking figures to the alert riflemen.

When the light of day erased the dark of night, the garrison was all set for an onslaught that did not materialize. There was still desultory firing by the Shawnees, but they seemed to be in no mood to press the attack. "This won't last long," Tip said. "Maybe they're expecting reinforcements. They have something in mind. But the longer they hold off, the better it will be for us."

About the middle of the morning the action of the Shawnees changed. Something had aroused them. They were seen flitting from tree to tree toward a common center in the woods. Two runners, zigzagging and running at full speed, reached the cornfield without being hit by the bullets from the fort. That they were preparing for an all-out attack was certain.

Tip ranged from one end of the blockhouse to the other, checking his riflemen. Little attention had been given to the back side of the fort. There was no cover between the buildings and the river. One man had been charged with watching for the enemy from that side. "Just keep cool and don't waste your shots," he warned the men at the portholes. "Shoot to kill, or not at all. Remember, there are three times as many Shawnees as there are men in this fort, but you have the advantage of cover, and they will have to come out in the open."

Soon more flaming arrows were lobbed at the fort. More Shawnees continued to dart from the woods to the cornfield, so that they would be closer to the stockade when the rush started. Most of them made it, but two of the darting targets were cut down by the riflemen in the fort.

The fiery arrows continued to fall. The dew, which had helped protect the roofs during the night, had dried in the morning sun, and the water poured on the roofs two days before had evaporated. They were dangerously dry.

Soon two fires sprang up on the cabin roofs. Ed Thomas and Tip climbed up from the corridor and doused them with water handed up to them, leaving some filled buckets on the roof in case they were needed later on. Then another fire sprang up on the roof of the end cabin, and Tip, who was nearest that end, carried a bucket over to put it out. The Shawnees were now keeping up a steady bombardment from the woods and cornfield. Tip was forced to go to the edge of the cabin roof to get near the fire. He had succeeded in quenching the flame when he collapsed from a bullet fired by an Indian who had raised his head and shoulders above the stockade and drawn a bead on Tip in his exposed position.

Tip slid down the roof and fell into the corridor, with a bullet through his hip. A shot from the blockhouse found its mark, and the Indian threw up his hands as he fell backward from the stockade.

Ed Thomas dropped down into the corridor and called for help. Heindrich Hoffer came down, threw Tip across his shoulder, and carried him into the blockhouse, where he passed him up to the men above. Mrs. Harris was ready with bandages. "Lay him on the table. I'll take care of him," she said.

Jan, from his station at one end of the fort, took note that some of the Indians were working around behind the stockade, with the probable intention of surrounding the fort and rushing it from all sides. More rifles had to be moved to the back side to keep a balanced defense. Indians were now dashing from the cornfield to the cover of the stockade. Someone cried, "There's another fire on the cabin roofs."

The defense was becoming confused. Tip, the symbol of authority, was out of action. Jan rushed into the middle room, where his mother was drawing a tight bandage to stop the flow of blood from Tip's hip. He grasped Chris's shoul-

der, "Move over to the back wall, Chris," he told him.

But Chris, in the wild excitement of the impending assault, had lost his usual calm reason. "Get over there yourself," he yelled. "Who are you to be giving orders?"

Jan hesitated an instant as he stepped back, then his fist shot out to catch Chris square on the chin. Chris crumpled in a heap. To Hoffer, who was staring in surprise at the action, Jan stopped long enough to say, "Throw some water on him, Mr. Hoffer. We need his rifle."

Norie, loading rifles at the table, had observed the action with some surprise, but never stopped her work for an instant. Jan's old smoothbore was one of the rifles on the table. Thrusting it into Norie's hands, Jan said, "You can shoot, Norie. Defend that back wall." Without question, she moved to the porthole indicated.

Again Jan heard the word, "Fire!" He sprang to a porthole and looked out to see the fire on the roof gaining headway. He looked around in desperation. His eye fell on young Donald MacGregor and Hughie Donlin. "You boys," he said, "go down into the corridor and up onto the cabins. You must put out the fire. There's no one else can be spared. There are some full buckets on the roof. Keep low, so you won't get shot, and don't waste the water."

He turned to find tall, strong Mrs. MacGregor standing before him. "Leave the fire to me, Jan, and go on with your work," she said. " 'Tis a fine job you are doin'. Come, laddies," she said to the boys.

The shooting from the outside was becoming a steady bombardment, and the yells seemed to be louder and nearer. Jan looked out to see what was taking place. More Shawnees were making their zigzag dashes from the cornfield to the stockade. A small, flaming brand fell at his feet. He looked up to see flames through a small, burned hole in the roof. At last the slab roof had caught fire. He hurriedly climbed the ladder to a platform that had been arranged under a hatch built in the roof, and twisted the bar loose that held the cover locked down. As he was about to raise the cover, Mrs. MacGregor climbed up from the lower room, followed by her two young helpers. "Come down from that, laddie," she ordered. "You have other work to do. I'll attend to the fire."

Jan dropped to the floor. He upended a table some four feet square and, with the small ax he carried on his belt, struck off the legs. "If you can handle this heavy top as a shield, Mrs. Mac-Gregor," he said, "one of the boys can carry a bucket of water while you both crouch behind it. Take off your shoes. Your bare feet will cling to the roof better."

When she climbed to the platform under the hatch, Jan handed up the table top. With no especial show of exertion, the brawny Scots-woman plucked the heavy table top from his hands. Turned diagonally across the opening in the roof, it barely slid through. Steadying it with one hand, she helped her eleven-year-old son to the roof with the other. "Stay behind the board, Donald," she directed, "and carry the water. I will shield you and myself as we slide over to the fire."

Feeling that the job of fire fighting could not be delegated to anyone more efficient and reliable, Jan hurried over for a look through the porthole. The Shawnees were piling over the stockade all along the line. In spite of the steady firing from the blockhouse, many were reaching the walls. Heindrich shoved his loaded rifle into Jan's hands. "Better you should use it," he said. He picked up one of the shotguns, loaded with buckshot, saying, "With this I do better."

Jan hit one of the charging Indians as he zigzagged up the slope. His mother put another loaded rifle into his hands. He slid the barrel through the porthole but could find no living target. Two of the Shawnees were draped grotesquely over the stockade, and two more lay on the slope. All the living members of the band had reached the walls. Off from the ell, he could hear the steady firing of Morris and Tyndal, as they tried to clear the Shawnees away from the area in front of the cabins.

Norie jerked at his sleeve. She said, "There are some Indians on the back side, under my station. They're setting a fire. The overhanging logs are so close together that I can't shoot down between them."

"Mr. Hoffer!" Jan called. "They're setting a fire against the back wall."

The Dutchman picked up an ax. "We'll have to go out the back door," he said. "This I will use."

Jan picked up one of the heavy horse pistols from the table and thrust it into his belt. He was worried about what was taking place on the roof, but had no time to find out. "Take a look up on the roof, Norie," he called, as he started below. "And bring some water," he said to Hughie Donlin. "We'll need it."

Unbarring the heavy door, Heindrich Hoffer swung it open. Not twenty feet away, three Shawnees had kindled a fire in a bundle of splinters. The flames were licking up the sides of the logs. Jan shot the nearest Indian through the head. Then Hoffer brushed him aside and charged the two remaining Indians with his ax upraised. They drew their tomahawks, but he was upon them in an instant. His ax came down and split the head of the nearest one. The other did not wait to engage this mountain of fury. He dashed away and disappeared around the corner of the building.

"Quick, Hughie, bring the water," Jan said, running to kick the blazing brands away from the wall. While Hoffer poured the water upon the burning logs, Jan cautiously peeked around the edge of the door, which had swung straight out from the building. There were four Shawnees along the wall behind the door, but no fire was in evidence. One of them raised his rifle and took a pot shot at Jan's exposed head. Jan felt the bullet cut through his hair, and blood came streaming down the side of his face. Just a scalp wound, he realized.

Hoffer had quenched the last licking flame. He

seemed utterly unmindful of danger. "Come in, Mr. Hoffer," Jan called. The bar dropped in place across the door as the Indians reached it.

Jan quickly scaled the ladder to the second floor. As he reached it, Norie called from the platform, "There are two Indians on the roof."

Without hesitating a moment, Jan picked up the other horse pistol from the table and climbed quickly to the platform. The fire was out, but one Indian was stalking Mrs. MacGregor, who was fending him off with the table top. She was keeping Donald between the table top and herself and the Indian below her on the slope of the roof. The second Shawnee was outflanking her. In a few seconds more one of their tomahawks would lay her low.

Jan debated only a moment which one he should shoot. He raised the pistol and shot the Shawnee farthest away in the chest. The Indian threw up his arms and slid headfirst off the roof. The other brave, a big man wearing a chief's regalia, grasped the table top with one hand and raised his tomahawk in the other. Jan hurled the heavy pistol at him. It struck his arm, deflecting the descending tomahawk so it only struck the Scotswoman's head a glancing blow. Mrs. Mac-Gregor made a mighty thrust with her shield against her foe, upsetting his balance on the sloping roof. He fell backward and also slid head-first to the ground.

Mrs. MacGregor caught Donald by the shoulder and hurried over to the hatch. " 'Tis a brave laddie you proved yourself with the fine help you gave your mother," she was saying.

"Help her down, Norie," Jan flung over his shoulder, as he descended the ladder two rungs at a time. "It's nothing serious," he assured his mother, when she gasped at the sight of his bleeding head. She thrust a rifle into his hands.

Morris came running from his station in the ell. "The Indians have broken into the end cabin," he cried. "They'll be streaming into the corridor any minute! We'll have to go down."

"Wait a minute," Tip said. "Something is happening over by the woods."

Jan ran to look out across the clearing. An

Indian had come out of the woods, waving his gun over his head and shouting something.

"He's saying, 'Go! Go!' " Tip said. Like all frontiersmen, Tip, in his dealings with the Indians, had picked up a few words of their language.

The war cries of the Shawnees died away. In a moment the entire force around the blockhouse was retreating swiftly down the slope and over the stockade. Few of the portholes were manned, since most of the men had answered the call to come below. But two of the Shawnees dropped as the band dashed in their zigzag manner across the clearing. Tip had reserved his last shot for the Indian who had come out of the woods—a long shot to the extreme end of the clearing.

The Indian dropped at the crack of the old marksman's rifle, but scrambled to his feet and staggered into the protecting timber.

Jan had attempted to count the Indians as they crossed the cleared ground. "The best I could count," he told Tip, "was that less than twenty-five got back to the woods."

"Less than half of them," Tip observed. "Now if you'll help me over to the table, Jan, I'd like to lie down. Then go out and tell the bunch not to stir away from the fort. Never can tell what Indians have in mind."

13.

"You'll Do"

When he went below, Jan found many of the company gathered in front of the cabins singing a hymn of victory, led by Mrs. Williams. He relayed Tip's warning about sticking close to the fort for the time being, then diffidently added, "Shouldn't we get busy cleaning up the mess upstairs just in case?"

Terry said, "I'll take a couple of men and make temporary repairs to the roofs. Morris, you and Ed had better stay on guard. The rest of you might go back into the fort and straighten things up."

Back in the blockhouse, Jan found that the battle had taken its toll. His mother and Mrs.

Tyndal were binding up Connie's arm, which had been hit by a bullet close to the shoulder. They told him how Connie had, in the stress of battle, sat on the edge of a table, loading the rifles with one hand while she held them clamped between her knees. Before the porthole he was defending, they found Doyle Donlin slumped against the wall, his rifle still on guard. When they stretched him out on the floor, they saw the bullet hole between his eyes. Mrs. Donlin was inconsolable. "Why did we come to this wild country?" she mourned. "And what will Hughie and I do without our man?"

Mrs. Williams put her arm around the grieving woman and raised her to her feet. "We pioneers fight together," she said, "and we live together. We'll look after you and Hughie. Come away with me now. The men will take care of Doyle."

The sun was five hours high, and an hour had elapsed since the Shawnees had disappeared into the forest. Morris called attention to something over at the edge of the clearing. "Looks like a handkerchief on a stick," he said. "That wouldn't be an Indian." A moment later someone rose from the screening cover, and the tall form of Trent came stalking, unafraid, across the clearing. A wild cheer went up when Tyndal said, "The Shawnees are really gone!"

When some of the men opened the gate in the stockade, Jan's mother ran out to meet Trent, hanging onto his arm with both hands, tears of happiness and relief from the strain of the past thirty hours in her eyes.

In answer to the many questions directed at him, Trent told them, "I reached Fort Nelson a couple of hours after daylight yesterday. This General Clark is a man of action. An hour later he had twenty well-equipped men in canoes. We made good speed down the river. I slept much of the day. It was dark when we landed a mile above where I had found the Shawnee's canoes. A sentry shot at two Indians, who came around our camp before daylight. Probably scouts left to watch the river."

"That accounts for the Indian who came to warn the Shawnees here," Jan said. "When will Clark's men get here, Trent?"

"Should be along in an hour," Trent answered. "I left them to find how matters stood here. I travel faster alone."

Mrs. Harris took Trent away to feed him. Everything about the settlement was assuming a normal air. The cabin doors were thrown open, and the scent of cooking was on the breeze. Jan went to wash away the blood from his wound and donned his one spare buckskin shirt. He wandered out and leaned against the ell of the blockhouse. The reaction from the action-packed hours of the attack had left him drained of energy. A vast lassitude possessed him mentally and physically.

Chris came by. He stopped to face Jan, and said, "I must have been out of my head up there in the fort a while ago. I guess you think a lot quicker than I do—hit quicker, too. I just want to say I'm sorry."

Jan shook his extended hand. "Let's forget it, Chris."

The two young pioneers stood looking out in silent contentment across the cleared space to the forest beyond—the forest they both loved and feared. Ed Thomas, with a message for Jan, found them there together. "Trent and Tip want you upstairs," he said.

Jan found Trent and his mother sitting on a bench beside the table upon which Tip was comfortably bedded down.

"How is your hip?" he asked Tip.

"Nothing to worry about," Tip told him. "Bullet missed the bone and passed right through. I'll be traveling again in a month." He paused, and then he said, "Jan, Trent and I want to thank you for warning us of the attack. And I like the way you kept a cool head today. I was watching you, boy. You'll do."

Jan could think of nothing to say in reply to so great a commendation from these seasoned scouts. His tongue refused to work.

Trent relieved his embarrassment by saying,

"I have something else important to talk about, Jan. I'm asking you for your mother."

Jan looked at his mother. Her face was lit up with happiness, though she looked a little anxious as she waited to hear what Jan would have to say. He drew himself up straight and answered gravely, as was appropriate when making a decision as the head of the family. "I shall be proud to see my mother married to you, Trent," he said.

The familiar little noises of domestic industry seeped up through the portholes from the nearby cabins. A feeling of calm serenity permeated the place. This was home.